# The Man in the Iron Mask

# STEP INTO CLASSICS™

# The Man in the Iron Mask

BY ALEXANDRE DUMAS
ADAPTED BY PAUL MANTELL

A STEPPING STONE BOOK™
Random House 🏠 New York

LIBRARY
FRANKLIN PIERCE COLLEGE
RINDGE, NH 03461

Copyright © 1998 by Random House, Inc. Cover illustration copyright © 1998 by
Bill Dodge. All rights reserved under International and Pan-American Copyright
Conventions. Published in the United States by Random House Children's Books,
a division of Random House, Inc., New York, and simultaneously in Canada by
Random House of Canada Limited, Toronto. Originally published as a Step into
Classics Book by Random House, Inc., in 1998.

www.steppingstonesbooks.com
www.randomhouse.com/kids

*Library of Congress Cataloging-in-Publication Data*
Mantell, Paul.
The man in the iron mask / by Alexandre Dumas ; adapted by Paul Mantell ;
cover illustration by Bill Dodge.
  p. cm.
"A Stepping Stone book."
SUMMARY: A simple retelling of the four Musketeers' final adventure during
which they plot to replace King Louis XIV of France with his twin brother,
the true king, who has been falsely imprisoned in the Bastille for eight years.
ISBN 0-679-89433-0 (pbk.) — ISBN 0-679-99433-5 (lib. bdg.)
1. Man in the Iron Mask—Juvenile fiction. 2. France—History—Louis XIV,
1643–1715—Juvenile fiction. [1. Man in the Iron Mask—Fiction. 2. France—
History—Louis XIV, 1643–1715—Fiction. 3. Prisoners—Fiction. 4. Brothers—
Fiction. 5. Twins—Fiction. 6. Adventure and adventurers—Fiction.]
I. Dodge, Bill, ill. II. Dumas, Alexandre, 1802–1870. Homme au masque de fer.
III. Title.  PZ7.M31835Man 2005  [Fic]—dc22  2004009646

Printed in the United States of America  18 17 16 15 14 13 12 11 10 9

RANDOM HOUSE and colophon are registered trademarks and A STEPPING STONE
BOOK and colophon are trademarks of Random House, Inc.

PARIS, SEPTEMBER 5, 1638

King Louis the Thirteenth of France stood on the palace balcony. He smiled down at the cheering crowd and held up his newborn son for all to see.

"Here he is!" the king shouted proudly. "Your future king, Louis the Fourteenth!"

Inside the bedroom, his queen cried out in pain. She was giving birth to another son—identical to the first!

The king came in and saw what was happening. "Oh, no!" he gasped. "Twins! One royal son is a blessing, but identical twins mean disaster for France. For when they grow up, they will fight over the throne. It will be civil war!"

The queen and her midwife, Perronnette, looked at each other in horror. What was the king going to do?

"I must think of my country first," he said sadly. "This second boy is just as much my son as the first. Nevertheless, he must disappear. No one must ever know that he exists. We will lock him in the dreaded prison of the Bastille. There he will remain hidden all his life."

"Please! No!" the queen begged. "There *must* be another way!"

"What other way can there be?" the king asked.

"He could grow up in the country, with no one to tell him who he is," the queen said. "Perronnette here can be his nurse. I will find a tutor for him. Our son will grow up to be a fine gentleman. He will never know he is ours, but at least he will have a happy life."

"All right," the king said. "But if he ever finds out…"

The queen nodded. She knew what he meant. If her poor son ever learned his identity, he would be dangerous to his brother. There would be no other choice but...the Bastille!

# Chapter One

*The years passed. The king died, and his five-year-old son became the next king, Louis the Fourteenth. The young king's mother and advisers ran the country while Louis grew up without a care. He was given everything he asked for and soon became very spoiled. By the age of fifteen, he was almost ready to ascend the throne. But he still knew nothing about his identical twin...*

Philippe lived at Chateau Noisyle-Sec, a beautiful country estate. Young Philippe's life was quiet and peaceful. He had everything he needed. He loved his home, with its gardens, fountains, and woods. He loved his nurse, Perronnette, and his tutor, Monsieur LaCoste.

But sometimes, he felt there had to be more to life. He was not allowed to go beyond the walls of the estate. He had never been out in the world.

Often, during meals or his lessons, Philippe felt that his nurse and tutor were hiding something from him. There were many questions they refused to answer.

"Am I a gentleman?" he would ask.

"Concentrate on your lessons, Philippe," would be the reply.

Or he would ask: "Who is the fine lady who comes here every few months and pays for my clothes and lessons?"

"She is a servant of your benefactor."

"What's a benefactor?"

"Someone who helps you."

"Who is *my* benefactor?"

"Your benefactor lives in Paris. Now eat your supper."

"And who are my parents?"

"I said, eat your supper, Philippe— and stop asking so many questions."

So it always went. Philippe knew he must be high-born, because the fine lady who came to visit was only a servant to his benefactor. If such people took an interest in him, he must be truly important. But who was he?

Philippe wondered if he would ever find out.

Then, one hot summer day, everything changed. Philippe was just coming back from horseback riding when he saw a carriage parked in front of the chateau. It was the fine lady from Paris!

Philippe came closer and stood behind a large tree. From there, he saw that the fine lady was talking with Perronnette and Monsieur LaCoste. With them was a tall man who was dressed as a priest.

Unseen, Philippe listened to their conversation.

"Are the boy's lessons going well?" the fine lady asked.

"Very well," said Monsieur LaCoste. "He is intelligent."

"And curious?" the priest asked suspiciously.

"No, Monseigneur Aramis," the tutor said. "He asks questions once in a while, as all boys will, but we never tell him anything."

"Good," the fine lady said. "And he is happy?"

"Yes, madame," Perronnette assured her. "Would you like to see him before you go?"

"We must be off," the priest said hurriedly. "Maybe next time."

"Meanwhile, here is our mistress's latest letter." The fine lady gave it to Perronnette. "Our mistress sends her regards. She thinks of the boy often."

Then the fine lady and the priest got into the carriage and drove off.

Philippe watched them go. He wondered who they were and what was in the letter.

A thunderstorm was brewing as Philippe took his horse back to the stable. Looking up, he could see his nurse and his tutor standing at an open upstairs window, reading the letter from his benefactor.

Suddenly, a gust of wind blew it out of their hands. The letter flew out the window. Monsieur LaCoste grabbed for it, but missed.

"Oh, no!" he cried, not seeing Philippe below. "The queen's letter!"

Philippe stood there, frozen. The queen! His benefactor was the queen of France herself!

# Chapter Two

Philippe could feel his heart pounding. He watched the letter as the wind blew it out over the courtyard. It came to rest on the edge of the well. Just as Monsieur LaCoste and Perronnette hurried outside, another gust sent it over the edge and down into the well!

Philippe hid behind a corner of the house and watched as they searched for the letter—in vain. When it started to rain, they gave up and went back inside.

Philippe went over to the well. It was dark and the rain was coming down in sheets. Philippe shivered. Quickly he grabbed the rope and lowered himself into the well.

The letter was on a ledge near the bottom. Philippe stuck it into his belt and climbed back up the rope. Then he hurried inside the warm house.

"Philippe, it's time for dinner," Perronnette called out.

"I'm not hungry tonight," Philippe replied. "I think I'll just go up to bed."

He went upstairs, closed the door of his room behind him, and lit a candle. Holding the letter up to the light, he read it:

*Dear M. LaCoste and Perronnette:*

*I send you my regards. Please continue to see that my dear Philippe grows to be a fine young gentleman. I will never forget you for the kindness you have done. Nothing is more important to me than Philippe's welfare— except, of course, the welfare of France. Here are my latest instructions...*

So! The queen of France cared deeply about him! Not only was she his benefactor, but he was dearer to her than anything except her country!

What could it all mean?

Philippe felt his head spinning. Dizzy, he collapsed onto his bed, still in his wet clothes.

By morning, he was in a high fever. Perronnette discovered him like that. As she tended to him, he talked in his sleep about what he'd read.

"The queen...my benefactor...cares about me...the queen...dearer to her than anything...but France..."

"He knows everything!" Perronnette gasped in terror. She realized what this could mean. Still, she and Monsieur LaCoste knew what they had to do. They were loyal subjects of the queen.

"We must write and tell her what has happened," the tutor said sadly. "It is our duty."

"But what will happen to Philippe?" Perronnette asked. "What will happen to us?"

The tutor sighed. "There is no other way," he said.

# Chapter Three

The queen's hand trembled as she read the letter. She stood before the fire-place with her closest adviser.

He was the priest who had gone to visit Philippe with the queen's servant. His name was Aramis, and he had once been a famous musketeer. He and his three friends, Athos, Porthos, and D'Artagnan, had once saved the queen's honor when she was young. Joined together by their motto—"One for all and all for one"—they had fought her enemies and defeated them.

Now the four musketeers had drifted apart. Athos and Porthos had retired to the country. D'Artagnan was the captain of the king's musketeers. And Aramis had become the bishop of Vannes.

"Oh, my lord bishop," the queen moaned, "what am I to do?"

Aramis stroked his beard and narrowed his eyes. "My lady," he said, "you have no choice. You must act for the good of the kingdom. The future of France is at stake!"

The queen sobbed and threw the letter into the fire. "Very well," she said. "I shall give the order. Philippe must spend the rest of his life locked in the Bastille!"

# Chapter Four

*Eight years passed. King Louis the Four-teenth had grown from a spoiled child into a bad king. Selfish and proud, he worried more about his money than about the people of France.*

*But Aramis had a plan—a plan that would help both him and France. For he knew a secret that could bring the king to ruin—a secret that lay hidden in the dun-geons of the Bastille...*

The king's court had gathered in the palace, as it did every morning. Dozens of servants, advisers, and guests crowded the hall, waiting for King Louis to enter.

In one corner of the room, two men stood talking. Once they had been musketeers in the queen's service. Now they were country gentlemen. They were visiting Paris to see the wonders of the big city and the palace.

One was a huge man, tall and strong. His clothes were old and out of fashion, but his heart was noble and true. His name was Porthos.

His companion, Athos, was not as tall or stout, but he was better dressed. The two musketeers had not raised their weapons in many years. But their swords still hung at their sides, a mark of rank and honor.

"Tell me, Athos," Porthos said, "who are all these people with their fancy clothes and phony talk?"

"They are the king's courtiers, Porthos," Athos replied.

"That one over there was very rude to me when I said hello," Porthos complained.

"His name is Fouquet," Athos told him. "He is the king's treasurer. All the money in France passes through his hands. They say a lot of it sticks to his fingers, too. He is the richest man in the kingdom—richer even than the king."

"Why doesn't the king just get rid of him?" Porthos asked.

"He may just do that," Athos replied. "Do you see that other man over there?"

"The one with the nasty frown on his face?" Porthos asked.

"That's him. His name's Colbert, and he's the king's chief adviser. He hates Fouquet and is trying to get rid of him."

"So much stealing and plotting!" Porthos said. "Whatever happened to old-fashioned honor? 'One for all and all for one'?"

"It's gone, my friend," Athos said sadly. "Nowadays, it's every man for himself. That's why I don't come to the palace much anymore."

"Look, there's D'Artagnan!" Porthos

said, waving to their old friend. "My, my, that's a nice uniform he's got."

"Good old D'Artagnan," Athos said with a smile. "He's still the same loyal fellow as always."

"And now he's captain of the king's musketeers!" Porthos beamed. "Good for him!"

"Yes, and good for France," Athos said. "Somebody's got to look out for the country."

"What about Aramis?" Porthos wondered.

"He looks after France, too, I think," Athos said. "But in a different way."

"Hello! Aramis!" Porthos called out, seeing him. "Will you look at him, Athos—a priest now, is he?"

"The bishop of Vannes, Porthos," Aramis corrected him, coming over to shake hands. "Hello, Athos. Porthos, old boy, where have you been?" he asked.

"On my farm out in the country," Porthos said proudly.

Aramis looked at his friend's old clothes. "Yes, I can see that," he said with a smile. "And now, if you'll excuse me, there's someone over there I need to talk to."

Aramis glided off and went over to speak with Monsieur Fouquet. He took the king's treasurer by the elbow and led him to a quiet corner of the room.

"Colbert is after you," he warned Fouquet. "He's trying to ruin your reputation with the king."

"I know it!" Fouquet moaned. "But what can I do, Aramis?"

"I have a plan, my lord," Aramis whispered. "You must invite the king and his court to stay with you at your new chateau, Vaux-le-Vicomte. Impress the king with luxuries. Wine and dine him, put on lavish entertainments. Dazzle him! That will make him favor you over Colbert."

"Do you really think it will work?" Fouquet asked.

"My lord, I am sure of it," Aramis replied.

Just then, the double doors at the end of the hall opened, and King Louis the Fourteenth entered. He had a thin mustache and was wearing a long wig of curly red hair. At his side was his elderly mother, the queen. Everyone bowed as Louis walked to his throne and sat down.

"First of all," he said, "we wish to extend a royal welcome to Athos and Porthos. You served our father and mother well, as did Aramis and D'Artagnan. We are forever grateful to you."

"Your Majesty!" Porthos said, bowing along with the others.

"And now," the king said to D'Artagnan, "what business comes before us today?"

"Monsieur Colbert wishes to speak, Your Majesty," D'Artagnan told him.

"Let him speak for all to hear," said the king.

The narrow-eyed, suspicious Monsieur Colbert came forward. He held a bunch of papers in his hands.

"Your Majesty," he said, "I can now prove that Monsieur Fouquet has stolen millions of francs from your treasury to build his chateau at Vaux. If you will look at these papers, sire?"

The king waved him off. "Monsieur Fouquet," he said. "What is your response to these charges?"

Fouquet stepped forward angrily. "Sire," he said, "I deny everything! It is a pack of lies invented by my enemies to destroy me!"

"You would say that even if you were guilty," the king said, scowling. "Anything else?"

"Yes, Your Majesty," Fouquet said. He glanced at Aramis. "I invite you and the entire court to stay with me at Vaux. There, you can judge for yourself if I am loyal and true to you."

"Very well," the king said. "We will

visit you at Vaux. It will be your chance to impress us with your loyalty and friendship."

Fouquet bowed and grinned at Aramis. He did not see the king turn and nod to Corbert, but Aramis did. His plan was working!

# Chapter Five

No moon lit the streets of Paris that night. The city was dark and cold. Mist swirled about the bishop of Vannes's carriage as it rolled along the deserted cobblestone streets.

This part of Paris was always quiet. An evil air hung over the neighborhood. It came from the fortress called the Bastille, the place where enemies of the king were imprisoned. Behind the Bastille's walls lay untold torments. Secrets so dark that to know them meant certain death.

The carriage pulled up before the prison gate, and out stepped Aramis. In his dark bishop's robes, he seemed a part of the night.

"Open the gates for the bishop of

Vannes!" the driver cried. And the doors swung open. Aramis stepped through.

"I want to see the governor of the Bastille," he told the guard.

"Right away, my lord bishop," the guard said with a bow. He ran off. Soon, the governor of the Bastille came waddling toward Aramis.

"Aramis! Or should I say, Lord Bishop!" he said with a bow.

"Baisemaux." Aramis returned the greeting. "It's been a long time…"

"…since our days as musketeers," Baisemaux said. "You've done well for yourself, eh?"

"Thank you. You haven't done too badly either, I'd say."

"Ugh," Baisemaux said, making a face. "It's all right running a prison, I suppose. But you should hear the poor devils at night, screaming and moaning about their innocence. It's enough to drive you crazy."

"Mmm," Aramis murmured, nodding. "I'm sorry to rush you, Baisemaux, but it's not you I've come to see."

"Oh!" Baisemaux said, taken aback. "No. Of course. I understand. Who is it you wish to see?"

"A prisoner by the name of Marchiali has asked me to hear his confession. I presume he wishes to clear his conscience."

"Marchiali? Oh, yes, I know him. A real gentleman, that one. All right, follow me, then." He led Aramis inside the prison. Ahead of them walked a guard with a ring of keys.

The three men's footsteps echoed on the stone steps as they walked down into the depths of the fortress. Here, in damp dungeons below the ground, were kept the most important prisoners, the ones with the darkest secrets.

The guard stopped at a heavy wooden door. He found the right key and unlocked it. Aramis turned to Baisemaux.

"You must wait out here," he told his old companion. "Confessions must be private."

"Well, it's against regulations," Baisemaux complained. "But seeing that you're a bishop, I suppose it'll be all right."

Aramis nodded and stepped through the door. He pushed it closed behind him.

It took a moment for him to make out anything in the darkness of the cell. He held up his lantern, and slowly, his eyes adjusted.

There, sitting on a stone bench, was the man he had come to see—the man who had been given the false name Marchiali.

He was young, with long brown hair, a thin mustache, and noble features. He looked sad, as though he had given up hope of ever getting out of here.

"Who...are you?" he asked Aramis.

"I am your confessor."

The prisoner sat up. "I have committed no crime," he said. "Therefore I have nothing to confess."

"Are you sure?" Aramis asked softly. "In the eyes of those in power, sometimes it is a crime simply to know that a crime has been committed."

"I don't understand," the prisoner said.

Aramis smiled. "You will."

"I thought prisoners had to request confessions," the man called Marchiali said.

"You did," Aramis said. "I arranged it." He glanced around the cell. Rats scurried away from the glow of his lantern. Moss grew on the damp walls. "I wanted to see you…in private."

"Then it is you who must confess to me," the prisoner said. "For surely you have come here to tell me something secret and of great importance."

Aramis nodded slowly. "If the king knew I was here, I would not see the sun rise tomorrow."

"I will listen," the prisoner said. "But tell me first who you are."

"You have seen me before," Aramis told him. "Do you not recognize me...Philippe?"

The young man stared at his visitor long and hard. "The man who came with the fine lady to visit me...that last time..."

"Yes. I am Aramis, bishop of Vannes. And you are the boy Philippe, all grown up—and a prisoner! Such an injustice!"

"What happened to my nurse and my tutor?" Philippe asked. "I've thought so much about them. They were so kind to me..."

"They are no more," Aramis told him. "Poison silenced their tongues."

Philippe gasped and fought back tears. "My enemy must be very powerful, and very cruel, to kill two innocent people and imprison a child."

"In your family, Philippe, they do whatever is necessary. Your existence had to remain a secret at all costs."

"But why?" Philippe asked, rising from his bench and facing Aramis. "Why am I here? I must be someone important to have deserved such treatment. Who am I, Monseigneur?"

"I will tell you," Aramis said. "But first, I must ask you two questions. In the house where you grew up, were there any mirrors?"

"Mirror?" Philippe said. "What's a mirror?"

"I thought not," Aramis said. "And did your tutor ever teach you about history?"

"Only about the early years of France," Philippe told him. "I always asked to learn more, but we never seemed to get to it."

"You were not meant to know," Aramis said. "History reveals the past, and mirrors show the present. You were shown neither. So now I must tell you what has been happening in France since the day of your birth."

Aramis told Philippe the story of the birth of the royal twins and the fateful decision to keep the second birth secret. Philippe listened, his mouth half open, his eyes staring into nothingness.

"And so the second son disappeared," Aramis finished. "Only his mother, the queen, knows that he exists."

"His mother, who didn't want him! His mother, who gave him up and sent him away!" Philippe said bitterly. "Yes, only his mother knows...and you, of course."

Philippe began pacing back and forth in the cell. Aramis watched as the full truth sank in.

"You, Monseigneur, knew the secret. Now you have chosen to reveal it to me. Tell me—have you a portrait of the king, my brother?"

"I do indeed," Aramis said, producing a small painting of Louis the Fourteenth and handing it to Philippe.

Philippe stared at it for a long time. "So…this is the face of my enemy," he finally whispered.

"And here is a mirror," Aramis said, holding it up for Philippe to see.

Philippe held the mirror up next to the portrait. Identical faces stared back at him.

"Now tell me," Aramis said, standing close beside him. "Which of the two is king?"

"He who sits on the throne," said Philippe, his anger boiling. "He is king. And there is nothing I can do about it. I am a prisoner, nothing more."

"I can make you more," Aramis said, reaching out a hand to grab Philippe by the shoulder. "If you truly desire it, I can make you king of France!"

"Please, sir," Philippe begged. "Don't tempt me with dreams of power if you cannot deliver them. I do not need to be king. To be happy, I only need to be free."

"Unless you tell me not to, *sire*, I

mean to go ahead with my plan."

"How can you overcome both my mother and my brother?" Philippe asked. "If they have put me here, how can you restore me to my rightful place?"

"Do not be weak or fainthearted, my friend," Aramis said, staring into Philippe's eyes. "I shall do as I have promised."

"And my brother? What will happen to him?"

"He has benefited from this great crime, while you have suffered. It is his turn to sit here in darkness, and yours to sit on his throne."

Silence filled the cell as the two men stared at each other. "I don't know..." Philippe said.

"Your brother is surrounded by corrupt, evil men. He listens to their advice, and France suffers for it. When you are king, you will choose someone else for your adviser. Someone who cares deeply about the future of France."

"Someone like you?" Philippe asked.

"I shall return, Your Majesty," Aramis said. He knocked on the cell door for the jailer to open it. "The next time I come, it will be to set you free."

Aramis bowed deeply, and Philippe returned the gesture. The door opened, and Aramis left the cell.

"That was the longest confession I've ever heard of," the jailer said. "He must have had a lot to be sorry about."

"Yes," Aramis said, "but not any-more."

# Chapter Six

The next day, Aramis paid a call on Monsieur Fouquet.

"How are things going, Fouquet?" Aramis asked him. "Everyone's buzzing about the great festival you're throwing in the king's honor. Are the preparations coming along all right?"

"Yes, they are coming," Fouquet said anxiously. "And the money is going. *My* money! I shall soon be ruined, unless this turns out as you say it will."

"Oh, do not fear, my friend," Aramis assured him. "On the day after the king's arrival at Vaux, you shall have millions, I promise you."

"Do you really think the king will be impressed?" Fouquet asked.

"He will be dazzled," Aramis said. "And he will see how much you love him."

"I hope so."

"Do not worry, Fouquet. And leave the money matters to me." Aramis got up and went to the window. He stared into the distance, where the towers of the Bastille rose above the city roofs. "And now, Fouquet, there is a favor I must ask of you," he said.

Fouquet looked at him. "A favor? You are doing so much to help me. What can I do to repay you?"

"I need a letter from you," Aramis said. "A signed order to free a certain prisoner from the Bastille."

"And which prisoner is that?"

"A man named Seldon," Aramis said. "He wrote two poems making fun of the king. And for this crime, he has spent ten years behind bars."

"Ten years for a couple of poems?" Fouquet gasped. "But that's terrible!

Why didn't you tell me about this injustice before?"

"I only just learned of it," Aramis lied. "His poor, sick mother wrote me a long letter, begging for his release."

"I will order it at once!" Fouquet said, beginning to write. "And I will give you this purse for the prisoner. In it are 10,000 gold francs from the king's treasury."

"That is very kind of you, monsieur," Aramis said, taking it.

"Yes, I am too kind, too generous with the king's money," Fouquet admitted. "That is my fault. I am a very poor banker, but my heart is good and true."

"The king will be sure to see that when he comes to Vaux," Aramis said. "How soon can you send the order to the Bastille?"

"Tonight," Fouquet said. "No later than nine o'clock."

"Very good," Aramis said. "Thank

you, monsieur. You are most kind. You will not be sorry."

"Tonight at nine," Aramis said to himself as he left the room, "I will be at dinner with my old friend, the governor of the Bastille."

# Chapter Seven

That evening at sundown, Aramis's carriage arrived at the Bastille. Aramis stepped out, and with him came a servant carrying a full case of fine wine.

"Fetch the governor!" Aramis ordered.

When Baisemaux arrived at the gate, he was pleasantly surprised to see his old companion. "I did not expect you again so soon!" he said as the two shook hands.

"You know, Baisemaux," Aramis said, "seeing you has made me miss our old friendship. And since I know how you always dine alone here, I decided to invite myself to supper. I've brought a little something with me to drink as well."

"You are more than welcome, old friend!" said Baisemaux, who really never had been close friends with Aramis. But Aramis was an important man. Besides, Baisemaux had seen the case of fine wine, and he was not about to turn down such a gift. "Come inside and dine with me! A pleasure! A real pleasure!"

"The pleasure is all mine," Aramis said, following his host inside. "Wait here for me," he told the driver.

The two men went inside to Baisemaux's quarters. They sat down together, and Aramis poured wine for both of them.

"I notice you're dressed as a musketeer tonight and not as a priest," Baisemaux said.

"Yes," Aramis replied. "I wished to remind myself of the good old days— one for all and all for one, eh?"

They toasted each other, and Baisemaux drank his wine in one gulp. But Aramis merely sipped his.

"Here, Baisemaux, let me refill your glass," he said slyly.

An hour later, the two men were in the middle of dinner. They were also on their fifth bottle of wine. Most of it had been drunk by Baisemaux.

Just then, a horse's hooves clattered in the courtyard below. Seconds later, a servant entered the room.

"Monsieur Governor!" he said. "A messenger has arrived with a letter for you!"

"Tell him to go away!" Baisemaux said. "Can't you see I'm eating supper? Whatever it is, it can wait till tomorrow."

"Pardon me for interfering, old friend," said Aramis. "But what if the message is important? Shouldn't you at least read it now?"

"Messages that arrive in the middle of supper…" Baisemaux complained. "Oh, well, if you say so, Aramis." He turned to the servant. "Have the message brought to me," he said.

The servant went out and returned soon after with a letter tied up in a scroll. Baisemaux opened it and read it.

"This is an order for the release of a prisoner, signed by Monsieur Fouquet!" Baisemaux frowned. "What nerve these powerful people have! They arrest a poor man just like that and put him in prison without a trial. They leave him there for years to rot. And then they want me to release him 'at once!' 'At once,' mind you! I call that nerve. The poor devil can surely wait till morning."

"No!" Aramis said, almost shouting. He quickly calmed his voice. "I may be dressed as a musketeer, but I am still a man of God. It would be wrong to keep this man in prison one moment longer than necessary. Release him now, and you will be rewarded in heaven."

"But we're not through eating," Baisemaux protested. "Oh, very well," he said with a sigh. "Since you ask me to do it, I will have him released at once."

Baisemaux staggered over to the door and called out for his servant. While his back was turned, Aramis took the letter and put it in his pocket. Then he drew out another letter and put it in the first one's place.

Baisemaux was at the door, talking to the servant. "Have the prisoner Seldon brought here. He is to be released at once."

"Pardon me, old friend," Aramis said. "But didn't you mean to say 'the prisoner Marchiali'?"

"Marchiali? No, the name is Seldon. It says so right there in the letter."

Aramis looked at the letter he had put on the table. "No, my friend. It clearly says Marchiali. See for yourself."

Confused, Baisemaux came back to the table and examined the letter. "Marchiali!" he gasped. "But I could have sworn…"

"Perhaps," Aramis whispered, "you have had a little too much to drink."

"Yes...perhaps I have," Baisemaux said, scratching his head. "I can't understand it...Marchiali...the man I am supposed to watch more closely than anyone..."

Suddenly, he swung around to face Aramis. "Wait a moment—he is the same prisoner you visited last night!"

"True, he is," Aramis agreed. "It *is* rather a coincidence, isn't it? Still, orders are orders. According to this letter, your orders are to set the prisoner free."

Again, Baisemaux scratched his head. "Orders are orders," he repeated. "Oh, well, I suppose you're right, Aramis." He turned to the servant. "Bring the prisoner Marchiali here at once!"

Soon, Philippe was brought into the room. His hands and feet were in chains, but when he saw Aramis, he couldn't help smiling.

"Unchain him," Baisemaux ordered, and it was done. "Young man, you are free," he said to Philippe. "You must swear never to tell anyone anything about this place. What you have seen and heard here must remain a secret forever. Do you swear?"

"I swear," Philippe said. "My time here is not something I wish to remember."

"Very well, then," Baisemaux said. "You're a free man. Congratulations. I must say I don't understand the order myself. But orders are orders, eh, Aramis?"

"Oh, yes, certainly," Aramis agreed, giving Philippe a secret wink.

"Where will you go at this hour of the night?" Baisemaux asked Philippe.

Before he could answer, Aramis stepped in. "I will take charge of the prisoner," he said. "I will help him with anything he may need." He gave Philippe a little nod of the head.

"Must you be going so soon?" Baise-maux asked Aramis. "We were just getting started on dinner!"

"I'm afraid I must go, old friend," Aramis said, embracing him. "But I'm sure we'll be seeing each other again soon. Yes…sooner than you can imagine."

# Chapter Eight

Outside, the carriage was waiting for them. Philippe was not accustomed to freedom. It made him so dizzy that Aramis had to help him get into his seat.

The carriage sped away. It headed for the countryside, stopping along the way at each of the city's many guard-posts.

Soon, they left the houses and lights of Paris behind. They passed farmlands and hills. Then they entered a stretch of dark, lonely woods. Aramis ordered the driver to stop the carriage.

"We need to talk," he told Philippe. "Would you prefer to stay in the carriage, or would you rather go outside?"

"I want to be out in nature again,"

Philippe said eagerly. "It has been years since I've seen it, and I love it so. Look! The night sky is so beautiful...and the trees...I am free! Free!"

"Your Majesty," Aramis said, "nature has given you the same face as your brother's. Up until now it has been a curse. Now it will become a blessing. We will take advantage of this 'gift' of yours. By the day after tomorrow, you shall sit on your brother's throne!"

"And he?" Philippe asked.

"He shall sit in your old dungeon cell," Aramis said.

"Won't he speak out?" Philippe asked.

"Whom will he speak to?" Aramis challenged. "The bare walls?"

"But surely someone will see that I am not the real Louis the Fourteenth!"

"Sire, you look like your brother, and you can act like him. No one will know the difference. Just learn to play your part, and all will go well!"

"Perhaps," the young man said. He stared off into the distance, and a sad expression darkened his face. "But...is it the right thing to do?" he asked. "My conscience stings me."

"Your *conscience?*" Aramis repeated.

"Yes. It tells me I owe loyalty to my brother."

"Your brother is in the grip of evil men, ministers like Colbert, who care only for themselves and not for France. This country needs a king who is honest and strong!"

"Like me?" Philippe asked.

"Yes! Your Majesty, you were born a prince. You have lived a life of misery! Is it not justice that you should have your turn on the throne?"

"And it is all thanks to you, Monseigneur. I owe you a great debt. How can I ever repay you?"

"When you are king—if you *choose* to be king—you will repay me handsomely," Aramis told him. "First, you will pay Fouquet's debts and allow him to retire in luxury. He is a good man, and he deserves forgiveness. Then you will dismiss Colbert and put me in his place as your chief adviser. Together we will rid France of corruption and restore the kingdom to health. Then, when you are fully established as king, you will make me the pope. The two of us will then rule the world together!"

Aramis saw that Philippe was still not convinced. He sighed deeply. "It is useless for me to share such a brilliant vision with a person who prefers to live in darkness," he said.

"It isn't that, my friend," Philippe said. "But we are different. You long for power. I've always lived a humble life. I don't need a kingdom to be happy."

"You have already said so," Aramis reminded him. "All right, the choice is yours. If it's a simple life you want—I know of a piece of land. There's a little house there and not many neighbors. You can hunt in the woods and fish in the streams. You can grow vegetables and raise chickens. I'll see that you have all the money you need to live a quiet, peaceful life..."

Aramis stared hard at Philippe, then continued. "Or you can sit on the throne of France and rule over a kingdom! Which is it to be, Philippe?"

"Allow me a moment to consider," Philippe said. "Then I will give you my answer."

"Very well," Aramis agreed, and stepped back inside the carriage.

Philippe walked a short distance away. He breathed in the nighttime country air and felt refreshed. Freedom was wonderful. He had missed it so.

He got down on his knees and prayed for heavenly guidance. Then he listened within himself for the answer to his question. When he arose, he knew what he had to do.

"Well?" Aramis asked, emerging from the carriage.

"Take me to where the throne of France is to be found," Philippe ordered.

"Sire!" Aramis bowed deeply. "Your wish is my command. And may I say, you will make a wonderful king—Your Majesty!"

He bowed low once more, then helped Philippe back into the carriage. "On to Vaux!" he told the driver.

As they went, Aramis handed Philippe a notebook. "Here," he said. "Study these notes, and you will learn all about everyone at the court. You must know them perfectly—all their little habits and ways—if you are to convince them that *you* are Louis the Fourteenth!"

# Chapter Nine

Chateau Vaux-le-Vicomte was the grandest estate in all of France, even more spectacular than the king's palace in Paris.

It had not always been that way. For years, Monsieur Fouquet had been spending millions to improve the mansion and its grounds. He stood now on the grand balcony with Aramis. The two men watched as the carriages of the king and his court approached the chateau.

"How proud you must be," Aramis said, "to have the king and his entire court come to visit."

"Proud?" Fouquet repeated. "I'm worried, Aramis. What if I fail to dazzle the king?"

"Oh, you will not fail, Fouquet. You have made this chateau the grandest in France. You have spared no expense preparing the food and entertainments for His Majesty. How could Louis not be impressed?"

Fouquet frowned. "He does not like me, Aramis. To tell you the truth, I've never liked him much either. But now that he is about to be my guest, I suddenly feel warm and affectionate toward him."

"Don't say that," Aramis said quickly. "Just remember, he is a spoiled young man. He has always lived in luxury. It takes something spectacular to impress him. And believe me, he is going to be impressed with Vaux."

"How happy it would make me to dazzle the king!" Fouquet said longingly. "If only he would change his mind about me..."

He sighed and turned to Aramis. "Anyway, I'm grateful to you for suggesting all this. You've always been helpful, Aramis. Remember when you suggested last year that I improve the guest rooms?"

"How could I forget?" Aramis asked with a smile. "I supervised the work myself."

"Yes, and as a result, the king's bedchamber is a thing of beauty. It's almost as if you knew he would be coming!"

"Yes, isn't it…?" Aramis agreed.

"Which room will you be staying in, my friend?" Fouquet asked.

"The blue room on the second floor," Aramis said.

"The room just above the king's? But why would you want to be in there? You couldn't make any noise at night, for fear of waking the king."

"I do not move around much at night," Aramis assured him. "Mostly, I read in bed until I fall asleep."

"But what about your servants?" Fouquet asked.

"I have only one, and he is a very quiet young man," Aramis said.

"I see," Fouquet said. "Well, suit yourself." Then he cleared his throat. "Er, Aramis...about those millions to repay the money I owe..."

"You shall have the money tomorrow, Monsieur Fouquet. You have my word on it. Now come. Let us go down and greet the king."

# Chapter Ten

The grand caravan of carriages arrived: King Louis and his servants, his mother, the queen and *her* servants, his advisers and *their* servants, his guests and *their* servants, not to mention D'Artagnan and a contingent of musketeers. But the chateau at Vaux was big enough for them all.

Dinner that evening was a magnificent feast. Thirty courses were served, cooked by the finest chefs. The most expensive wines were drunk from golden goblets encrusted with jewels.

Everyone seemed to be having a fabulous time. Everyone, that is, but the king. Louis the Fourteenth ate silently, never smiling. Fouquet saw that the king was not happy.

"After dessert," Fouquet announced, "we shall have a ballet and fireworks in honor of our sovereign, Louis the Fourteenth!"

Everyone applauded. But Louis stood up and said, "I am tired. Fouquet, lead me to my bedchamber."

"But, sire, the entertainments..." Fouquet protested meekly.

"I merely wish to rest for a few minutes," the king explained. "All the day's traveling has made me tired."

"Very well, Your Majesty," Fouquet said, "right this way. The entertainments will just have to wait."

He led the king out of the banquet hall and down the corridor to a set of double doors carved with golden angels.

"This is your room, sire," Fouquet said, opening the door to a huge round room with a domed ceiling. Painted on the ceiling were angels and clouds. Below them stood an enormous, soft bed.

"This room is called the Chamber of Morpheus, the god of sleep," Fouquet said. "The famous artist LeBrun painted the ceiling. That's Morpheus up there, surrounded by the angels."

"A masterpiece," the king admitted. "It must have cost a fortune. Your chateau is quite grand, Fouquet."

"Thank you, sire!" Fouquet said. "My home is your home!"

"Hmm," said the king, narrowing his eyes. "Yes...Leave me now, Fouquet. I wish to be alone. Wake me when it's time for the fireworks."

"Yes, sire." Fouquet left, and the king lay down on the bed and closed his eyes.

Above him, on the ceiling, the face of Morpheus moved!

# Chapter Eleven

Philippe stared down at the king through the hole in the floor. Below him, the king lay in bed with his eyes closed.

Just then, a knock came at the door. "Open," Aramis's voice said. "It is I."

Philippe replaced the painted face of Morpheus in the spy hole, then got up and opened the door.

"Have you been studying the king?" Aramis asked.

"I have," Philippe said. "And I have memorized all the notes you gave me."

"Good. All is going according to plan. The king is jealous of Fouquet's wealth, as I knew he would be."

"But I thought Fouquet was our friend!"

"He is…in a way," Aramis said.

"You mean he does not know?" Philippe was astonished.

"Not yet," Aramis admitted. "I will tell him soon. For now, though, you must hide in the closet. My friends, the musketeers Athos, Porthos, and D'Artagnan, are coming up for a visit."

Philippe went to the closet and made sure the peephole in the door was open.

"That's it," Aramis told him. "Study them and learn their ways. It will help you when you are pretending to be Louis."

Soon, the musketeers were sharing stories of the old days. Before too long, Athos went downstairs for some fresh air. Porthos fell asleep and began snoring loudly.

"He never changes," D'Artagnan said with a smile. "Good old Porthos—a truer friend there never was."

"Yes," Aramis said, a secret smile crossing his lips. "One never knows when one shall need a true friend."

D'Artagnan's eyes narrowed. "Aramis," he said suspiciously, "you're up to something. Don't tell me you're not—I'm never wrong about these things."

"It's true, old friend," Aramis said. "Your instincts are the best in all of France."

"Well, what is it, then? If you're plotting against the king, you know I'll stand against you."

"I would never plot against the rightful and true king of France," Aramis answered slyly. "Believe me, D'Artagnan—he has no better friend than Aramis."

"So it is Colbert you're against? In that case, you can count on my friendship. Colbert is only loyal to himself."

"I agree," Aramis said. "So if the king should dismiss him and appoint someone else—someone more honest—to be his chief adviser, you would support that?"

"With all my heart," D'Artagnan said. "And now, we must be going. The evening's entertainments will be starting soon."

"I'm afraid I shall have to miss them," Aramis said with a sigh. "Like Porthos here, I am tired and ready to sleep."

"Very well, then," D'Artagnan said. "See you in the morning." With that, he bowed and left the room.

As soon as he was gone, Philippe opened the closet door. "I'm worried about D'Artagnan," he told Aramis. "I think he suspects something."

"Yes," Aramis said. "D'Artagnan is like a loyal dog. He has a good sense of smell. But if he thinks you're his master, he'll do anything for you. And by tomorrow, sire, he will think you are his master."

"I see."

"Now go back into the closet. I must wake Porthos and speak with him. For he, too, has a part to play in our charade."

"Porthos? But—"

"Shh. Just watch."

Philippe went back into the closet, and Aramis shook Porthos.

"Wake up, old friend!"

"Hmm? What is it? What's happened?"

"Nothing's happened yet, but something terrible is about to happen—unless you and I prevent it."

"Tell me!" Porthos cried.

"First I must swear you to secrecy."

"I won't tell a soul! Upon my honor!"

"Very well, then," Aramis said. "Porthos—the very throne of France is at stake!"

"The throne of France? Lead the way, and I shall defend it!" Porthos said, standing up and taking out his sword. "I may be old, but I can still fight. One for all and all for one, eh?"

"Yes, yes," Aramis said. "But put away your sword for now, Porthos. You must act for the moment as if nothing is wrong. Go downstairs and enjoy the entertainments. Then, at midnight, you will meet me in the cellar."

"I'm your man!" Porthos said in a whisper. "I serve the king of France, and will fight like a champion to protect him!"

"Your loyal service is sure to be rewarded," Aramis said, smiling. "I'm sure the king will make you a count, or even a duke, for this!"

"A duke! Well, now! Just think of it!" Porthos strode proudly out of the room, and Aramis closed the door behind him.

Philippe emerged from the closet again. Aramis removed the piece of floor and stared down through the peephole.

"Look!" Aramis said to Philippe. "The king is talking with Colbert. Come and watch!"

The king seemed very angry. "This Fouquet lives even more grandly than I do," he said to Colbert. "Who does he think he is?"

"Your Majesty," Colbert said, "ask yourself where Fouquet gets all the money to pay for this splendor."

"And what is the answer?"

"He gets it from *your* treasury, sire. I have the papers to prove it!"

"Good, Colbert! We shall seize his possessions and send him to the Bastille! Then everyone will know I am greater than he!" Louis stood still, his fists clenched in the air. "Now come, Colbert, let us go see these fireworks. Tonight will be Fouquet's last night of glory!"

When they were gone, Aramis turned to Philippe. "Colbert is a liar and a snake," he said. "Much worse than Fouquet." Then he smiled. "But after tonight, everything will be different. Everything!"

# Chapter Twelve

The grand ballet was magnificent, but the fireworks were even more spectacular. Everyone was impressed. But King Louis was boiling with jealousy and anger.

When the entertainments were over, he turned to his servant and said, "Tell D'Artagnan to meet me in my chamber in five minutes!"

When D'Artagnan entered the Chamber of Morpheus, the king turned to him and said, "I want you to arrest Monsieur Fouquet at once!"

D'Artagnan was stunned. "But, sire!" he protested. "How can you arrest a man who has spent every penny he has to entertain and please you?"

"Every penny he has? It is *my* money,

*France's* money, that Fouquet has been spending. Arrest him, I say!"

"But, Your Majesty, is it right to arrest him while you are a guest in his house?"

"I may be a guest, but I am also the king, and the king is master wherever he goes!"

"To arrest him now would bring disgrace on you, sire," D'Artagnan said. "People will say it is shameful and not worthy of you."

D'Artagnan knelt before the king. "At least wait until afterward, when you are back in Paris. Think it over, Your Majesty, and perhaps you'll even change your mind—"

"I will *not* change my mind!" the king shouted. "I hate Fouquet! He is a thief who thinks he is greater than the king—and he shall pay dearly for it!"

But then the king seemed to reconsider. He sighed and sat down on the bed. "Oh, very well, I'll think about it.

But only overnight! Keep Fouquet under guard for now and come see me in the morning for further orders."

"Yes, Your Majesty," D'Artagnan said. He got up, bowed, and went to the door. "Good night, sire. Sleep well, and have pleasant dreams."

# Chapter Thirteen

When D'Artagnan had gone, the king lay down on the bed, exhausted. Too much excitement had made him tired and dizzy. Even now, he thought he could see the face on the ceiling moving. The eye of the painted Morpheus, god of sleep, seemed to be winking at him.

Louis rubbed his eyes and stared at it. No, it couldn't be. He must have imagined it. He was tired...so tired... Soon his eyes closed again, and he was asleep, dreaming...

In his dream, the face of Morpheus gazed down at him. It was a face so like his own that it was practically identical. The face grew smaller, farther away.

Now the bed seemed to be moving too. Louis felt himself sinking slowly downward, downward, into his dream. The face on the ceiling grew still more distant. He saw it now as if through a long, dark tunnel. All around him, a humming noise filled the air.

Louis tossed and turned in bed. A feeling of danger filled his mind and body. What was happening to him?

Suddenly, the bed jerked to a stop. The humming ceased. Louis felt a coldness, a dampness in the air. He told himself to wake up...forced himself to sit up...

"Come, it is only a dream," he told himself, staring at the stone walls that surrounded him.

But it was no dream. For Louis had his eyes fully open. He had gone to sleep in his bedchamber and now found himself...where?

Suddenly, two masked men stepped from the shadows.

"Who are you?" Louis asked, terrified. "Is this some sort of joke?"

The two men came closer. One was a huge fellow, the other tall and thin. It was the thin man who spoke. "It is no joke, sir. You must come with us."

"Fouquet sent you, didn't he?" the king gasped.

"It doesn't matter who sent us," the thin man replied. "You must do as we say. Now get up at once!"

"I am the king of France!" Louis shouted.

Now the huge man spoke. "You ought to be ashamed for daring to impersonate the king!"

"What? I am the king, I tell you!" Louis insisted.

"Silence!" the thin man commanded. "We are your masters now!"

"If you mean to kill me, do it now and get it over with!" Louis demanded.

"Never mind that. Just get up and get going!"

Louis got up and walked between the two masked men. They headed down a long, dark tunnel that led to a door. The thin man opened it, and the three of them stepped out into the night. They were in a patch of woods just outside the gates of the chateau. Before them stood a carriage, ready and waiting.

"Where are you taking me?" Louis said.

"You'll soon find out," the thin man replied.

The three men sat down inside the carriage. Soon, they were riding through the woods and farmlands, speeding toward Paris.

Behind them, in the chateau of Vaux-le-Vicomte, in the Chamber of Morpheus, the elevator mechanism reversed itself. The grand bed, now empty, rose back up into its former place. Philippe stood beside it. It was he who had pressed the button that had activated the machine. Now he took Louis's wig of long, curly red hair and placed it on his own head. He took from his pocket the portrait of his brother that Aramis had given him. He looked up at the full-length mirror on the wall.

*Perfect,* he thought. From this moment on, he was no longer Philippe. He, and only he, was Louis the Fourteenth, King of France!

And his brother, who until this moment had been the king? Philippe shut his eyes tightly and tried not to think about him.

Slowly, Philippe climbed into the king's bed and tried to sleep. Thoughts raced through his mind: fears, hopes, dreams. Would he be able to fool the court? His ministers? His mother? And, above all, would D'Artagnan, with his cunning instincts, see through the masquerade?

Philippe went over, for the thousandth time, all that he had learned about the king's manners and habits. He had seen the king for only a few brief moments from the room above. But now he had to be that person all day long, every day, for the rest of his life!

Aramis had assured him that he would get used to it in time. Philippe hoped that was true. For now, he was excited but afraid. When the sun rose, his new life would begin—or end!

# Chapter Fourteen

Two hours after it had left Vaux, the carriage containing the real king pulled up at the gates of the Bastille. Out stepped the two masked men. The thin one shut the carriage door behind him. Then he removed his mask. It was Aramis.

"You can take that mask off for the moment, Porthos," he told his companion. "But you'd best stay here, just to make sure the prisoner doesn't escape."

"He won't escape me, I can assure you!" Porthos declared, putting his hand on the hilt of his sword. "I may be old, but I'm not too old to serve my country and my king!"

"Good old Porthos!" Aramis said, clapping his friend on the shoulder. "France is indeed lucky to have a defender like you."

Then Aramis went up to the guard at the gate. "Fetch the governor of the Bastille," he told him. "I have a prisoner to return to him."

Five minutes later, Monsieur Baisemaux appeared, rubbing his sleepy eyes. "Monseigneur the bishop!" he said, surprised to see Aramis. "What are you doing here at this late hour? I did not think to see you again so soon! Not that it isn't the greatest pleasure—"

"Baisemaux," Aramis interrupted, "I am returning the prisoner Marchiali to your care. As you suspected, the order for his release was a mistake. It was Seldon who was supposed to go free after all."

"I told you so, didn't I?" Baisemaux asked. "Oh, my goodness, this will be the end of me!"

"Not at all," Aramis told him. "Marchiali is inside my carriage. Once he is back in his cell, it will be as if this incident never took place. No one will be the wiser."

"Are you sure?"

"Yes. Don't worry." Aramis put an arm around Baisemaux's shoulder and whispered in his ear. "My old friend, may I share a secret with you? Will you promise not to breathe a word of it?"

"I will guard your secret with my life!" Baisemaux swore.

Aramis nodded, then spoke. "As I'm sure you have noticed, this Marchiali looks quite a bit like His Majesty King Louis."

"I've noticed, all right," Baisemaux said. "I always suspected that was why I was ordered to watch him so closely."

"You were right, my friend," Aramis said. "Marchiali poses a great danger to the state. The moment he was free, he used his liberty to try to impersonate the king!"

"No!" Baisemaux gasped.

"I'm afraid so," Aramis said sadly. "Even now, he keeps insisting that he is Louis the Fourteenth. He is quite out of his mind, I'm sorry to say. Just ignore his ranting."

"I certainly will!" Baisemaux promised.

"You know, the king is furious about this," Aramis confided.

"Oh, no!" Baisemaux groaned. "Does he blame me for the mistake?"

"He did at first," Aramis lied. "But I explained to him that it was an honest error. For now, he will overlook it. But be sure you don't let Marchiali out again. He must never even be allowed to speak to anyone!"

"Of course not!" Baisemaux agreed. "Oh, I do hope the king will understand. Come—let us drag this wretched criminal back to his dungeon cell!"

Aramis put on his mask again, and signaled Porthos to do the same. Then he opened the carriage door.

King Louis stepped from the carriage and looked about him. "The Bastille!" he gasped. "I see. You men are the most wicked of traitors to your king and country! When my mother, the queen, hears of this, she will have you beheaded!"

"Shut up!" Baisemaux shouted.

Turning to the guards, he added, "Shoot him if he speaks again!"

He shoved Louis toward the gate. "Not another word out of you!" Then he led the king of France into the Bastille and toward the cell where his brother had languished for so many years.

Meanwhile, Aramis and Porthos got back into the carriage and removed their masks. "You have saved France yet again, my friend," Aramis congratulated Porthos.

"My love for my king is boundless," Porthos said solemnly. "For him, I would risk everything!"

*You already have, old friend,* Aramis thought. *You already have...*

# Chapter Fifteen

The jailers led the king of France down the slippery stone steps to the dungeon. There, they shut him up in his cell. The thick oak door slammed, and he was alone.

"I am the king of France!" he shouted. The walls echoed his cry. "Do you hear me? I am the king of France! Release me at once! I am the king, I tell you!"

Rats and mice scurried to and fro, looking for a hole to hide in. The king gasped in horror and shrank back against the wall. Never in his life had he been so close to such horrid creatures!

He paused to catch his breath. Slowly, his heartbeat returned to normal. King Louis looked about him. He was in a small, narrow room, with a high, high ceiling. Way up one of the walls was a tiny window. A shaft of moonlight beamed through it—the only light in the cell. *What would it be like in here on a moonless night?* he wondered.

There was a wooden table and chair, and a stone bench cut into one of the walls. Louis went over to the bench and lay down. His head was still spinning. It was almost as if he were dreaming. Perhaps this whole horrible experience had been a nightmare and nothing more!

But no. It had really happened. And Louis was certain that Fouquet was behind the whole evil plot!

Louis frowned. When he was free again and sitting on his rightful throne, he would take care of that scoundrel Fouquet! No longer would that criminal live in luxury at France's expense! Louis would take over all Fouquet's property—including the grand chateau at Vaux. And Fouquet would sit here, in the dungeon of the Bastille!

Louis looked about him again, at the very real cell he now occupied. "I am still a young man," he said softly to himself. "Yet they will leave me here to rot for the rest of my life."

Suddenly, it hit him—this cell was to be his home forever!

"No!" he screamed. "No! I am the king of France! This cannot be happening to me! Somebody help me! Help! Help!"

Nobody responded. He wondered if the guards could even hear him through that thick oak door.

"Help!"

The echo of his cry vibrated in his mind, until it seemed it would never stop. Louis rose to his feet, grabbed the wooden chair, and smashed it against the door. It splintered into pieces. He grabbed one of the legs and began pounding it on the door. "Get me the governor!" he shouted, banging and banging. "I want to see the governor of the Bastille!"

No one opened the door. But the noise woke some of his neighbors. Louis could hear them now, calling to him from the other cells nearby.

"I am innocent!"

"Help me!"

"I want to see the king!" cried one prisoner. "I know I can convince him he was wrong to put me here! Let me speak with the king!"

Louis was stunned. These were men *he* had put here! And for what? He remembered dozens of times when he'd had men arrested for tiny little wrongs—writing poems or songs making fun of him or saying nasty things about him to a friend or neighbor. For crimes like those, he, Louis of France, had put them here in this horrible dungeon!

None of these men were ever going to get out, Louis realized. They were stuck here for the rest of their lives. As king, he would never have pardoned them. Every time someone at the palace had tried to talk to him about freeing prisoners, Louis had always said no.

Well, Louis swore to himself, if he ever got out of here, that would change. If he ever got to be king again, he would be a true king—better than he had been.

He would begin by freeing all these prisoners from the Bastille. Whatever they had done, surely they had suffered enough. And in their place, he would put that criminal, Monsieur Fouquet!

As for Colbert, *he* would follow the king's wishes, and not the other way around. Louis was determined to take charge of France and lead her to glory. If only he could get out of here!

In another fit of desperation, Louis threw himself against the door and pounded on it with his fists. He dug his nails into the wood, screaming for the guards to come and set him free. He rolled on the floor, pounding his head on the stones in fury.

By the time the guard came with

some food and water, King Louis of France was unrecognizable. So when he greeted the guard with "I am the king of France!" the guard replied, "Sure you are. You don't even look like him!"

"But I *am* him! I am Louis!"

"King Louis is a grand gentleman with fancy clothes," the guard pointed out. "You're nothing but a beggar wearing rags. Your face is filthy and your eyes are wild. I'm not listening to you. Here, eat your supper and leave me in peace."

"I'm the king of France, I tell you!" Louis insisted, tearing at his hair in frustration. "Listen to me. They've kidnapped me and thrown me into prison. You must help me! France's future is at stake!"

"I can see you've gone out of your head," the guard said. "I'd better take away this knife and fork. You'll have to eat with your hands."

The guard stood in the open door and looked back at the prisoner.

"Funny," he said, "you never used to make such a fuss when you were here before."

And with that, he shut the door.

"Wait!" Louis screamed. But it was too late. He heard the key turn in the lock, and the guard was gone.

In a blind rage, Louis took his plate of food and threw it across the room. The plate broke into a thousand pieces, and the food scattered on the floor. The rats and mice edged out of their holes, smelling their dinner.

Unaware of them, Louis was lost in thought. Something the guard had said...

"I was quieter when I was here before?" the king repeated to himself. "But...I've never been here before in my life! What in the world did he mean by that?"

# Chapter Sixteen

At dawn, there was a soft knock on the door of the Chamber of Morpheus. Philippe sat up in bed with a start. He had finally dropped off to sleep just a minute or so before. He had dreamed of men coming to get him in the night. Had they come for him now? Come to drag him back to the Bastille?

He cleared his throat and tried to calm himself. "Who's there?" he asked in the tone of voice he'd heard the king use.

"It is I, Your Majesty, the bishop of Vannes," came the familiar voice of Aramis.

"Come in, my friend," Philippe said. "My only friend," he whispered softly to himself.

Aramis entered the room, followed

by a servant. The servant held three suits of clothes for the king to choose from: one red, one green, and one purple.

"What would Your Majesty care to wear today?" the servant asked.

"The...the purple one, I think," Philippe said nervously. "Yes. Now go. I wish to speak with the bishop."

"Wouldn't you like me to dress you, Your Majesty?" the servant asked, confused.

Philippe remembered from his notes that he was supposed to let the servants do everything for him. "Oh. Yes, of course. Dress me. But hurry."

When the servant had done his duty and left, Aramis spoke to the king. "How did you sleep, sire?" he asked.

"Not well," Philippe said. "Is it done?"

"It is done," Aramis replied. "He will not trouble you again."

"You have done well," Philippe said. "And now it is my turn. I hope I can play my part as well as you have played yours."

"I am sure you will do splendidly," Aramis said. "You certainly look the part. Now you have only to act it, and France will be yours to command."

At that moment, there was a knock at the door. "That will be D'Artagnan," Philippe said. "The king—I mean, my brother—told him to come at dawn for orders about Fouquet."

"He must not see you just yet," Aramis warned. "D'Artagnan's senses are the keenest in France. If he comes into this room, he will know that something happened here last night. It is better not to let him see you until you appear before the entire court. No, you stay here. I will take care of D'Artagnan for the moment. And of Monsieur Fouquet as well."

Aramis opened the door and slipped out, shutting it softly behind him. Philippe sat back down on the bed. He wondered what Aramis was up to now.

# Chapter Seventeen

"Aramis!" D'Artagnan's face was the picture of surprise. "What are you doing in the king's quarters at this early hour?"

"The king cannot be disturbed right now," Aramis said.

"But he asked me to come first thing this morning," D'Artagnan said.

"The king did not sleep very well last night, and he is feeling out of sorts," Aramis explained.

"I see," D'Artagnan said, a suspicious look on his face.

Aramis ignored it. "However, he asked me to tell you that he has changed his mind about Monsieur Fouquet. He is to be set free at once."

"Well!" said D'Artagnan. "That's a relief. To arrest a man while one is a guest in his house did not seem right to me."

"I'm glad you think so, old friend," Aramis said. "I heartily agree. In fact, I think I'll come with you to Monsieur Fouquet's room to see his joy when he hears the news."

The two men walked together down the hall and up the stairs to Monsieur Fouquet's quarters.

"I did not know, Aramis, that you and the king were such good friends," D'Artagnan said as they went. "I've only seen the two of you speak once or twice. How did you get to be such a favorite of his?"

"You are mistaken, good D'Artagnan," Aramis assured him. "The king and I have spoken hundreds of times about important matters of church and state. But he has sworn me to secrecy about our conversations. Do you understand now?"

"Oh, yes," D'Artagnan said. "Now

that you put it that way, I understand perfectly."

But he did not understand. Not at all. Not yet. Then and there, D'Artagnan swore to himself that, whatever was going on, he would get to the bottom of it.

Monsieur Fouquet's face turned white with fear when he saw the two men enter his room. "A priest!" he gasped in fear. "Have you come here to hear my last confession? Am I condemned to die, then?"

"On the contrary," D'Artagnan said. "We have come here on the king's orders to set you free!"

*"What?"* Fouquet looked from one to the other. He could not believe King Louis would change his mind so completely and so suddenly.

Aramis spoke. "As I told you it would, Fouquet, your feast in his honor has won you the king's favor. He now thinks of you as a true and loyal friend."

"I will leave you now so that I may attend to my duties," D'Artagnan said. "I am happy that the king has decided to forgive you."

When he had gone, Aramis turned to Fouquet. "Well? Have I not been a true friend to you, Fouquet?" he asked. "You are free, you have been pardoned, and you shall have the millions I promised you—enough to pay all the money you owe and to live comfortably for the rest of your days."

"It is a miracle," Fouquet said, sighing with relief. "And you are indeed a true friend, my lord bishop. But I can't understand it—last night, the king sent D'Artagnan to have me arrested. This morning, he sends D'Artagnan to set me free. What does it all mean?"

In response, Aramis turned and locked the door. He went to the window and drew the curtains. "I will tell you what it means," he said in a low voice.

"The king suspects you of stealing from the public treasury. He is jealous of your wealth and the splendor of your home. He hates you and thinks you have betrayed him."

"But—but then why is he setting me free?"

"Do you seriously believe King Louis would set you free?" Aramis said. "The king is your deadly enemy! Don't you know that?"

A look of dread came over Monsieur Fouquet's face. "What is this all about?" he asked. "You are hiding something from me. What is it? What is between you and the king?"

"The king and I share a secret that no one else knows," Aramis said slowly. "A secret that will change the future of France."

"You frighten me," Fouquet said. "What is this terrible secret? Out with it at once!"

"Very well, you shall hear the truth,"

Aramis said. Then and there, he told Fouquet all that had happened, from the birth of the royal twins to the events of the night before.

When he had finished, Aramis stood silently, watching to see the reaction to his words. He expected Monsieur Fouquet to be surprised—shocked, even. But in the end, Aramis was sure the man would go along with his plan. After all, the real king would have thrown Fouquet in prison. The new king had set him free and pardoned him.

But Aramis, for once, had made a serious mistake. He had not counted on Monsieur Fouquet's sense of honor.

*"What?"* Fouquet cried angrily. "You have had the king kidnapped and imprisoned while he was under my protection? While he was a guest in my house?"

"Because of my actions, your house is still your own. If not for what I did, you would now be in prison!"

"How dare you, sir?" Fouquet said, fuming. "You have blackened my good name forever! I shall never forgive you for this! Never!"

"Sir," Aramis said, beginning to grow nervous, "please remember that, by putting the king in prison, I have saved your life. You ought to be grateful for the service I have done you."

"*Grateful?* My life and property mean nothing to me next to my honor! And you have taken it from me, you wicked man!"

"All that I have done, I have done for you, monsieur," Aramis said.

"Perhaps that is true," Fouquet said, "but I did not ask you to do it, I did not want you to do it, and I will not forgive you for doing it!"

"But, monsieur—" Now it was Aramis's turn to go white with dread.

"I reject your services, Aramis. Now leave my house at once and never return! Because you have been a friend to me, I will give you four hours to escape the king's revenge. Now go, if you wish to save your life! As for me, I am going to free my king!"

Fouquet hurried from the room, leaving a stunned Aramis behind. How could his brilliant plan have turned to ashes so suddenly, so unexpectedly?

All was lost, he could see that plainly. He would have to flee immediately. Perhaps he would go to Spain…he had friends there. And of course, he must take Porthos with him.

But what of Philippe? Could Aramis really leave him behind to suffer his fate alone? If he and Porthos took Philippe with them, sooner or later there would be civil war in France. The two brothers would fight for the throne, and the country would be ruined.

No. That must never be, Aramis decided. Whatever else was true about him, Aramis had always loved France. Whatever crimes he had committed had been for the good of France. He would not betray his country now. He would go to Spain and find his fate. Philippe would have to look out for himself. If the worst happened...well, Philippe had been a prisoner once. Perhaps he was fated to be one again.

# Chapter Eighteen

D'Artagnan was standing on the balcony of the chateau when he saw Aramis and Porthos gallop away on horseback.

"Hmm," he thought. "If I did not know better, I would say that those two were running for their lives. I wonder where they're off to?"

Just then, the horses turned, and Aramis and Porthos waved good-bye to their old companion. D'Artagnan waved back. In that moment, he had the feeling that he would never see his friends again.

A minute or two later, Monsieur Fouquet came out the front door of the chateau and stepped into a waiting carriage. "To Paris!" D'Artagnan heard him tell the driver. "The king is in danger!"

*The king is in danger?* D'Artagnan wondered what Fouquet meant. This morning, Aramis had said the king did not wish to be disturbed. Now Fouquet was off to Paris because of some unknown peril to the king.

D'Artagnan frowned. He was a man of action. Every one of his fine-tuned senses was telling him that now was a time for action.

But what was he supposed to do? The king had given him no orders. All he could do was wait. Soon, the king would assemble the court for the day's business. D'Artagnan would attend the session and keep his eyes open.

King Louis the Fourteenth did not see the dawn come. His eyes were closed as he knelt in prayer in his cell.

A sudden commotion outside his cell broke his concentration. Opening his eyes, he shouted, "Help! I am the king of France! I must speak to the governor! Fouquet has had me kidnapped!"

Louis's heart leapt with joy when the door flew open. Then it sank again. Standing before him was none other than his worst enemy—Monsieur Fouquet!

"Have you come to kill me?" Louis asked.

Fouquet stared at the king as if he'd seen a ghost. Louis's clothes were tattered rags, his face was smeared with dirt, and his hair and eyes were wild.

Fouquet looked at his king with sorrow and pity. "Sire," he said, "you have so few true friends. Don't you recognize one when you see one?" He went down on one knee and kissed Louis's hand. "Your Majesty, I am your faithful servant. I have come to set you free!"

Louis was astonished. "But wasn't it you who kidnapped me?"

"I? Never!" Fouquet said. "No, it was

the bishop of Vannes. He plotted to remove you from your throne and replace you with another."

He told the king the whole story of Aramis's plot to have Philippe take Louis's place. Louis listened, growing angrier by the minute.

"So. The bishop of Vannes, eh?" he finally said. "We shall deal with him! He and this impostor, Philippe. They shall pay for this crime with their lives!"

"But, sire!" Fouquet protested. "You cannot take the life of a royal prince of France! It would be an even greater crime than the one Philippe has committed!"

Louis stared at Fouquet as if he were crazy. "You do not seriously believe this nonsense about my having a twin brother, do you?"

"I do believe it, sire," Fouquet said. "In fact, I am sure of it. Philippe of France is your twin. You must not shed his blood. It would mean a public trial.

Then everyone in France would hear how your mother, the queen, sent her own child away to the Bastille. It would bring shame upon the throne of France!"

"Hmm…perhaps you are right," Louis said. "Fouquet, you have shown yourself to be a true and loyal friend."

"Thank you, sire," Fouquet said, bowing.

"However," Louis went on, "you have not been a good treasurer of France. When I have regained my throne, I will dismiss you from your high position."

"Yes, Your Majesty," Fouquet said. "I have failed in my task. It is fair and just that I retire from office."

"Good. And now," Louis said, getting up, "we shall return to Vaux and deal with these vile plotters. But first, we must stop at the palace so I can bathe and dress. When I appear at Vaux, I must look like my old self again."

They left the cell together and came

to the front gate of the Bastille. There, Baisemaux was waiting for them with a small group of armed guards. "Just where do you think you're going, Monsieur Fouquet?" he said. "As I told you, I have orders not to allow this prisoner to leave under any circumstances."

"And as I told you," Fouquet replied, "if you don't let him out, I shall return with an army and set him free by force!"

"Er, well, when you put it that way..." Baisemaux mumbled, stepping back. "Could I at least have a letter of release? If the king finds out I let this prisoner go, it could mean my life."

"Of course," Fouquet replied. "Sire, would you give him the letter?"

"Sire?" Baisemaux repeated. "What are you talking about?"

Louis signed the order of release and handed it to Baisemaux. "There," he said. "There is your letter." He stepped into the carriage, followed by

Fouquet. It sped away toward the palace.

Baisemaux shook his head in confusion. "First they let him out. Then they lock him up again. Then they let him out again..." He looked down at the order of release and gasped in astonishment.

It was signed "Louis the Fourteenth of France."

## Chapter Nineteen

"All rise for His Majesty, Louis the Fourteenth, king of France!"

Philippe heard the court herald announce his name—his *new* name—and knew it was time for him to enter the grand hall. Everyone would be looking at him. Would they be fooled?

He had prepared himself for this moment all morning, and now there was no holding back. Philippe stepped into the room and waved to the crowd of people.

They all bowed low and smiled at him as he passed, and said, "Your Majesty." Philippe returned the bows with a nod of the head, walked to his throne, and sat down.

Philippe was greeted first by Monsieur Colbert. "Your Majesty," he said, "I must say I was surprised that you decided not to arrest Monsieur Fouquet after all."

"I shall deal with Fouquet in my own way, Colbert," Philippe said in a commanding voice.

"Yes, sire," Colbert said meekly. "As you wish."

Philippe stuck out his chin and gazed around the grand hall. Everyone was looking at him with respect and affection. Clearly, no one suspected a thing!

Then Philippe's mother, the queen, entered the room. Philippe stared at her as she approached the throne. Ever since Aramis had told him the secret of his birth, he had hated the queen. It was she who had ordered him shut up in the Bastille.

Yet now, face to face with her for the first time, Philippe found that he could not hate her after all. She was so old—

much older than he'd imagined. Clearly, she was also sick. She moved very slowly, supported by a lady-in-waiting who held her arm as she went.

Philippe bent and kissed her hand. "Mother," he said. He looked deeply into her eyes.

"Louis," she said, frightened by his gaze, "why do you look at me like that?"

"I forgive you...Mother," Philippe said softly. "I forgive you for everything."

The queen's eyes filled with tears. "What...what are you talking about, Louis?" she asked.

"Never mind," Philippe said. "It is nothing. Nothing at all." She had given him away the day he was born. But Philippe also remembered her letter to his caretakers. She had declared that he was more important to her than anything else except France.

Except France...So it was for France's sake that she had done it.

Philippe was beginning to understand.

He cleared his throat and turned to the rest of the court. "Where is Monsieur Fouquet?" he asked.

"Sire," D'Artagnan said, stepping forward, "Monsieur Fouquet has gone to Paris. He said it was on account of some danger to your person."

"Danger to me?" Philippe repeated. "What sort of danger could that be?" Nervously, he looked around for Aramis.

"Where is the bishop of Vannes?" he asked. "I wish to see him at once!"

"Your Majesty," D'Artagnan said, "Aramis has fled."

"*What?*"

"He and Porthos rode away on horseback. They seemed in a great hurry to get away."

"But...but why?" Philippe gasped. He felt himself grow dizzy, and he sank back onto his throne.

Suddenly, there was a sharp knocking at the door. "Open up!" shouted a voice from the other side. It was Monsieur Fouquet's voice!

"Let him in," Philippe ordered.

The door opened and in walked Monsieur Fouquet—but he was not alone. Behind him came Louis, dressed, by sheer coincidence, in a purple coat just like the one his brother wore!

There was an uproar in the hall as people saw the two identical twins together for the first time.

The queen screamed as if she had seen a ghost. She staggered and was helped into a chair by her lady-in-waiting.

"Don't just stand there," Louis shouted. "Arrest that impostor!"

"Well, what are you waiting for?" Philippe asked the musketeers who were in the hall. "Seize that man!"

The crowd stood frozen, not knowing whose orders to obey. Louis turned to the queen. "Mother, don't you recognize your king?"

Philippe stepped toward her as well.

"Mother," he cried, "don't you recognize your son?"

The queen sobbed into her handkerchief, shaking her head miserably. Louis could see she was not able to act. He turned to D'Artagnan.

"Sir!" he said. "I leave it to you. Which of us is the king? One of us has spent eight years in the Bastille—his face must surely be paler than the other's!"

D'Artagnan stepped toward Louis and examined his face closely. Then he walked over to Philippe. Placing his hand on Philippe's shoulder, he said, "Sir—you are my prisoner!"

Philippe and Louis stared intently into each other's eyes. Then Louis lowered his gaze. He now knew how Philippe had suffered for his sake. Perhaps he felt guilty. He turned and quickly left the hall.

"Monseigneur," D'Artagnan said, taking Philippe by the arm, "I am sorry to have to do this. But I am a musketeer, and my oath of loyalty is to the king. I must place you under arrest until the king decides what to do with you."

"I understand," Philippe said, nodding. "Lead on, and I will follow."

D'Artagnan led him out of the room. As Philippe passed, everyone bowed their heads, in sadness and in respect.

# Chapter Twenty

That night, D'Artagnan entered the room where Philippe was being held under guard. He knelt before Philippe and removed his hat. "Your Highness," he said, "the king has decided your fate."

"Am I to die, then?" Philippe asked. "If that is to be my fate, I am ready."

"Here is the order," D'Artagnan said, handing him a piece of paper. "Read it for yourself."

Philippe took it and read: "The prisoner is to be taken to the fortress on the island of St. Marguerite. There, he will spend the rest of his days. His face will be covered with an iron mask, which he may never remove on pain of death. Signed, Louis the Fourteenth of France."

Philippe sighed deeply and handed back the order. "It is justice," he said. "I dared to usurp the throne. I take full responsibility." He turned to D'Artagnan. "Where is the mask?" he asked.

D'Artagnan went out of the room and returned a moment later, carrying the heavy iron mask. "I am sorry, Your Highness," he said. "Truly I am."

He lowered the mask over Philippe's head and locked it in place.

"You have shown yourself to be worthy of a crown," D'Artagnan told Philippe. "In your suffering and in your acceptance of your fate, you are truly noble. You are as much a king as your brother...perhaps even more so."

He bowed and kissed Philippe's hand. "Long live the king!" he said.

Philippe took from his pocket the portrait of his brother. He stared once more at his brother's face.

"Yes," he said. "Long live the king!"

*King Louis was a changed man from that day forward. He took full control of the kingdom and brought France to greater glory than it had ever known. To this day, people speak of him as the "Sun King."*

*To celebrate the kingdom's glory, he built the fabulous palace of Versailles, grander even than Fouquet's chateau at Vaux. It is still considered the finest palace in the world.*

*And what of the man in the iron mask? Over the years, his story has been told countless times. In the years following the events of this story, many people claimed to have seen a prisoner wearing a mask over his head to hide his identity. But no one ever saw the face behind the mask.*

*To this day, no one can say for sure if Louis's twin brother really existed, or if it was just a story.*

*What do you think? Is it only a legend? Or was there really a Man in the Iron Mask?*

**Alexandre Dumas** was born in France in 1802. He wrote several great novels and plays. Many of the characters in his stories were based on real people.

Dumas is best known for writing *The Count of Monte Cristo* and *The Three Musketeers*. He later wrote two more books about d'Artagnan and his fearless friends: *Twenty Years After* and *The Viscount of Bragelonne*. Dumas died when he was 68 years old.

**Paul Mantell** is the author of many books for children. He began reading classics as a teenager, and still enjoys reading them today. Paul lives in northern New Jersey with his wife, Avery Hart, and their two sons.

Do you want to read another exciting
Musketeers adventure? Then try

# The Three Musketeers

by **Alexandre Dumas**
adapted by **Deborah Felder**

D'Artagnan was in a rage as he headed for the staircase. Suddenly, a musketeer came out of a door near the landing. D'Artagnan ran headlong into him. The musketeer cried out in pain.

"Excuse me. I'm in a hurry," d'Artagnan said without stopping.

He started down the stairs. But a hand grabbed his belt and he was forced to stop.

"That is no reason for you to run into me, young man," said the musketeer.

"I didn't do it on purpose, sir," d'Artagnan said, recognizing Athos. "Now please let me go."

"You're not polite, sir," said Athos.

"Well, *you're* not going to give me a lesson in manners," fumed d'Artagnan.

"No? Then perhaps I can give you a lesson in dueling!" said Athos.

"I'm ready to fight a duel with you! Just tell me where and when," said d'Artagnan.

"Behind the Carmelite convent at noon," Athos said. He let go of d'Artagnan's belt.

"I'll be there," said d'Artagnan. He raced down the stairs.

Porthos and a soldier stood at the front door. D'Artagnan darted through the small space between the two men. But a gust of wind lifted Porthos' long velvet cloak. D'Artagnan ran straight into the cloak and became tangled inside the folds.

"Are you a wild man?" cried Porthos as d'Artagnan struggled to free himself.

D'Artagnan finally untangled himself. "Excuse me, sir," he said, looking up at the gigantic musketeer. "But I'm in a hurry."

"Do you close your eyes when you're in a hurry? You need to be taught a lesson!"

"And who is going to teach it to me?" d'Artagnan asked angrily. "You?"

"I, sir!" cried Porthos. "Behind the Luxembourg Gardens at one o'clock!"

"At one o'clock, then," said d'Artagnan. He dashed through the courtyard into the street. He looked around. But there was no sign of the nobleman.

"What a scatterbrained idiot I am!" he muttered to himself. "It was very rude of me to run out of Monsieur de Tréville's office like that. And now I must fight two duels with musketeers! If I survive, I will remember to be more polite in the future."

Just then, he saw Aramis talking to three guards. He bowed deeply to the musketeer. Aramis nodded at d'Artagnan and continued to talk to the guards.

D'Artagnan was about to move on. Then he saw Aramis drop his handkerchief and step on it. D'Artagnan bent down and pulled the handkerchief from under Aramis' foot.

"I believe that you have lost your handkerchief, sir," he said politely.

Aramis turned red. He grabbed the lacy handkerchief from d'Artagnan's hand. The scent of perfume filled the air.

"Aha!" cried one of the guards. "A gift from one of the queen's ladies-in-waiting, Aramis? Tell us about her."

D'Artagnan saw that he had embarrassed Aramis. "I'm sorry, sir," he said. "I hope you will excuse me."

Aramis glared at him. "I will not excuse you, sir," he said coldly. "A gentleman does not step on a handkerchief unless he is trying to hide it. Any fool knows that."

"How dare you call me a fool," cried d'Artagnan. "Draw your sword, sir!"

"Not here! Meet me at Monsieur de Tréville's house at two o'clock. I know a place where we can cross swords."

"My sword will be ready," said d'Artagnan.

It was almost noon. D'Artagnan headed for the Carmelite convent to meet Athos.

"The duel must be fought," he told himself. "But if I am to be killed today, at least I'll be killed by a musketeer."

When d'Artagnan reached the field behind the convent, Athos was waiting for him.

"My seconds should be here any moment," said the musketeer. "They will make sure we fight a fair duel."

"I have no seconds," d'Artagnan said. "I just arrived in Paris today. But it will be an honor to cross swords with you, sir."

"Thank you," Athos said with a bow. "I'll use my left hand to fight. The wound in my right shoulder is very painful."

"Then perhaps you'll let me give you an ointment," said d'Artagnan. "My mother made it. It heals any wound in three days."

"You are very kind. If we don't kill each other in this duel, I feel sure we shall become good friends. Ah, here come my seconds now!" said Athos.

D'Artagnan turned and stared at the musketeers. "Porthos and Aramis are your seconds?" he said in a surprised tone.

"Of course! We are always together. Everyone calls us The Three Musketeers."

Porthos and Aramis came closer and saw d'Artagnan. "What's *he* doing here?" cried Porthos.

"This is the gentleman I am to duel," said Athos.

"But I have a duel with him, too!" said Porthos.

"And so do I," said Aramis.

D'Artagnan drew his sword. "Then let us begin. On guard, Monsieur Athos!"

Just as the two swords touched, a group of the cardinal's guards came toward them. They were led by Monsieur de Jussac.

"Put away your swords quickly!" called Porthos.

But it was too late. "Stop, you musketeers!" shouted Jussac. "You're under arrest for breaking the cardinal's law against dueling!"

"There are five of them against three of us," Athos said quietly. "But I'd rather die here than face our captain after another defeat by the guards!"

"There are four of us, not three," said d'Artagnan. "It's true that I don't wear your uniform. But I have the heart of a musketeer. And I want to prove it."

"You're a fine boy," Athos said. "What's your name?"

"D'Artagnan, sir."

"Then Athos, Porthos, Aramis, and d'Artagnan will fight together! Forward!"

The four of them lunged at the cardinal's guards. D'Artagnan found himself face to face with Jussac. He fought like a tiger. Soon he had wounded the leader of the guards.

Within minutes, the musketeers had killed two guards and wounded the third. The fourth guard surrendered.

The musketeers and d'Artagnan helped the wounded man to the convent steps. Then, arm in arm, they all marched down the street together. They greeted every musketeer they met along the way.

D'Artagnan felt proud and happy as he walked with his new friends. He was on his way to becoming a musketeer!